# PARTY GIRLS POPSTARS

## Jess: Rave Reporter

# PARTY GIRLS POPSTARS

## Jess: Rave Reporter

### Jennie Walters

illustrated by Jessie Eckel

*h*

*Hodder*
*Children's*
*Books*

a division of Hodder Headline Limited

Another one for Laura,
with thanks for all her help

Copyright © 2002 Jennie Walters
Illustrations copyright © 2002 Jessie Eckel

First published in Great Britain in 2002
by Hodder Children's Books

A Catalogue record for this book
is available from the British Library

ISBN 0 340 85410 3

Typeset by Hewer Text Ltd, Edinburgh
Printed and bound in Great Britain by
Bookmarque Ltd, Croydon, Surrey

Hodder Children's Books
a division of Hodder Headline Ltd
338 Euston Road
London NW1 3BH

# POP FACT FILE:
## JESS

Pop faves:

StarStruck – the best band
   ever!

Copying dance routines from
   the TV

Reading pop mags

Sticking posters all over my
   room

Pop hates:

   Weird heavy metal groups
      like Legendary Dogz

Pop hobbies:

   Playing the drums

   Being a top pop fan!

Top pop gear:

Logo T-shirts

Badges

Glitter hair gel

Tinsel 'ears'

1

'I wish this lot would shut up!' Jess grumbled to her friend Sunny, looking round the classroom. She'd overslept that morning and missed breakfast; being hungry always made her grumpy.

It was pouring with rain, so the class was spending break indoors. Mrs Thomas, their form teacher, had just popped out to the staffroom and everyone was making the most of their freedom while she was away. A group of girls clustered around Emma Marshall were shrieking with laughter every five seconds while she read out messages from a paper fortune-teller. Jess felt as though her head was about to explode.

'Come on,' she decided, jumping up and grabbing Sunny by the arm. 'Let's make a move before Taffy comes storming back and blows her stack.'

They nipped down the corridor to see what their three other best friends – Caz, Lauren and Michelle – were up to. This classroom was a million times quieter than theirs; probably because Mr Maclaren was hovering around to keep an eye on things instead of puffing away on a ciggy in the staffroom like Mrs Thomas.

Lauren was drawing on a piece of paper, her head propped up on one elbow, while Caz and Michelle flicked idly through a magazine together on the other side of the table. Jess and Sunny sat down next to them and huddled around to have a look too.

'Great – a quiz!' Michelle said, putting a hand over Caz's to stop her turning the page. 'I love them. "Are you a party princess or a stay-at-home Cinderella?" Let's answer it together.'

'Come off it! Those quizzes are such a waste of time,' Sunny yawned. 'It's so obvious how you're meant to answer.'

'Well, I think they're a laugh,' Michelle said. 'And this is my magazine, Sunny, so tough! Right, first question – "Is your idea of a perfect party: A) dancing the night away to the latest tunes at a disco; B) going with a whole gang of mates to the cinema or a pop concert; or C) watching *You've been Framed* on TV with your mum?"'

'Hey, talking about pop – that reminds me!' Caz said suddenly. 'How could I have forgotten to tell you? Guess what arrived in the post this morning? Our tickets!'

'What tickets?' Lauren asked, looking blank.

'Our tickets to the roadshow, of course!' Jess yelled, leaping up. 'Oh, fantastic! I thought they were never going to come!'

And then they were all jumping up and down, making so much noise that Mr Maclaren had to call out, 'Steady on, you lot! What's the excitement? You sound like a herd of wild elephants!'

Jess and her friends had been looking forward to the roadshow for what seemed like months, ever since Caz had spotted the advertisement for it in a pop magazine. When they'd found out that some of their favourite bands and celebrities would be appearing, there was no way they were going to miss out. The tickets were quite expensive, but Jess had some pocket money saved up and she'd promised to wash her mum's car for the next few weekends to earn the rest. Caz's stepsister Natalie (who was eighteen and not half as scary as she looked) had said she would take them, and that was good news too.

Jess was the first to admit she didn't have a great singing voice, but she loved listening to pop music on the radio and copying dance steps from the videos on TV. Her favourite group was called StarStruck, and she had posters of them all along the wall next to her bed. There were two girls and three guys in the band. The boy she liked best was Marc, who had piercing blue eyes and dark curly hair. She'd scribbled his name all over the inside of her school bag and stuck his picture on her English file. Shona, her fave girl, had wavy auburn hair that  looked a bit like Jess's own (except that it was much prettier, of course). Sometimes she used to daydream about Shona being her perfect older sister; they would swap secrets and clothes and go shopping together, or maybe to the cinema.

Unfortunately, Jess's real-life older sister was Claire, who was thirteen and a complete pain. She had a twin brother, Matt, who was in Mr Maclaren's class along with Caz and the others (though she generally ignored him at school), and an older brother too: Eddie, who was really cool. He never minded her playing on his drum set and usually helped her if she got stuck on some tricky rhythm. Jess loved drumming. She'd had a few lessons, though it was difficult to practise with the drum kit being in Eddie's room. He'd promised her that she could have the drums when he went away to college, and then she'd take it up seriously. In the meantime, it was great to put her favourite CDs on Ed's stereo system when he was out, drum along to the beat, and imagine herself on stage with some funky group.

Jess sighed. 'I can't wait to see StarStruck,' she said, slumping back down in the chair with a dreamy expression on her face. 'I bet they'll really know how to get everybody up on their feet and dancing.'

'I think Highway 101 are way better than StarStruck,' Michelle said. 'The boys are really good-looking and their songs are wicked!' She hummed a few bars. 'I can't get "Waking Dreams" out of my head.'

'Miche! Are you crazy?' Jess was outraged. ' "Waking Dreams" must be the worst song that's ever been written! It's only got to number seven in the charts. And they don't even dance to it, they just sway about looking stupid.'

'That's because it's a ballad,' Michelle retorted. 'And they *don't* look stupid!'

Luckily, the bell interrupted this argument before it could become too heated. Jess was miles away in a world of her own. How could she possibly be expected to concentrate on lessons when there were so many other, fantastically more exciting things to think about?

'So, have you decided what to wear on Sunday?' Michelle asked Jess as they sat in the back of the car a couple of weeks later, going home from school. Michelle lived a few doors away in the same street as Jess and her family, so they usually shared lifts together. It was Friday afternoon – and the roadshow was only two days away!

'My black trousers, I think,' Jess replied. 'With that "Diva" T-shirt I bought a couple of months ago. How about you?'

'The denim dress Mum got me for my birthday.' Michelle had it all worked out. 'And I've seen this amazing sparkly cowboy hat in Glitterbug, though I don't know if I'd have the nerve to wear it. Can you come shopping tomorrow afternoon and tell me what you think?'

'I'll have to ask Mum,' Jess said quietly, pulling a kind of 'Don't want to push my luck at the moment' face behind the back of the front seats. Her mother was hunched over the steering wheel as she drove, muttering impatiently at everyone else on the road. She was a piano teacher, and Jess knew she was worried about getting home before her first pupil arrived. Friday afternoons were always a rush.

'I'm sorry to break into this cosy little chat,' Mrs Fitzgerald said, squeezing through a traffic light on amber, 'but you and Claire are cooking supper tonight, Jess. Remember? It was Matt and Eddie's turn last week.'

Matt turned round from the front passenger seat. 'And we're not doing it again, so don't even *think* about making up some pathetic excuse.'

'Oh, Mum! Do we have to?' Jess groaned. This was the last thing she felt like doing – and the last person she'd have chosen to do it with. She and Claire were fighting even more than usual at the moment, ever since Claire had discovered that her favourite band, Legendary Dogz, was appearing at the roadshow. Of course, all the tickets had been sold weeks before and Claire was furious about missing out. When she realised that Jess and her friends were going to the gig – well, it was as though they'd planned it just to spite her.

Jess couldn't understand why anyone would want to go and see Legendary Dogz in the first place. They looked horrible – shaven-headed, pierced everywhere and covered in tattoos – and their music sounded like cats fighting. Claire said it was a blend of metal, punk and hip hop. Whatever that was supposed to mean.

'Yes, you *do* have to!' Mrs Fitzgerald snapped, changing gear with a wrench. 'This is what we all agreed, Jess – remember? I have lessons back-to-back on Fridays, so you lot are doing your bit by helping with the cooking. Besides, it's a very useful skill to have up your sleeve. You can learn from Claire.'

'Huh!' Jess snorted at the idea. The only thing she'd learn from Claire was how to slam her bedroom door so hard it bounced back open, or tell someone what she thought of them with one withering look.

'I'll ring you later,' Michelle whispered. 'About the shopping.'

'If I'm still alive,' Jess muttered. 'Claire's probably planning to mug me for my roadshow ticket.' And that conjured up such a funny image that they both started giggling.

Jess was in too good a mood to feel cast down by anything for long – not even the prospect of a sticky cooking session with her older sister. After all, she was going to have a great day out with her friends on Sunday and Claire wasn't, so she was the lucky one. She could afford to turn the other cheek.

Later that evening, Jess was ready to kill. When it was time for them to start cooking, Claire had drifted into the kitchen and bossed her about for a while, telling her how to chop the onions and what to do with the mince. Then she'd had a call from one of her friends on her new mobile phone, and had gone up to her room 'for some privacy'. That must have been half an hour ago now, and Jess had been struggling in the kitchen on her own ever since.

She'd soon discovered that cooking bolognaise sauce was no easy matter. The mince stuck to itself in claggy lumps, however viciously she prodded it with a wooden spoon, and then the stupid ring pull snapped off the can of tomatoes. While she was searching for a tin opener, her carefully chopped onion charred into a thick black layer on the bottom of the pan, under the lumpy mince. And when at last she managed to slop the tomatoes into this unappetising mess, they bubbled ferociously and sent tiny crimson globules spitting back in her face.

She thundered upstairs to Claire's room, too furious to worry about keeping quiet for her mum's music lesson. Why should she have to suffer while Claire was gassing away to her friends? She flung open her sister's bedroom door to be greeted by a sight which made her angrier than ever, if that were possible. Claire was lying on the bed, reading a book. She'd finished her phone call, and hadn't even bothered to come back downstairs!

'What are you *doing*?' Jess spluttered, almost lost for words. 'Why aren't you helping me?'

'I've told you before,' Claire began, sitting up on the bed, 'don't come in—'

'I don't care!' Jess shouted, bright red in the face with injustice and rage. 'I don't give a monkey's about not being allowed in your stupid bedroom! I've been slaving away on my own down there, while you lie on your bed like a lazy – fat – slob!'

11

She grabbed Claire's legs and tried to drag her off the bed. 'Why should you always get away with it? You can come and do something for once, you mean – ugly—'

'Get off me!' Claire shrieked, thrashing about to try and dislodge Jess's grip. She threw her book down on the floor, and then suddenly they found themselves in the middle of a real fight. A hair-pulling, face-scratching, screaming, red-hot fury kind of fight.

It would have gone on a lot longer if two things hadn't happened. Firstly, Jess pushed Claire backwards so hard that she fell against the bedside table and sent her lamp, a pile of books and an alarm clock crashing to the floor. Secondly, their mother appeared in the doorway. The expression on her face stunned them both into silence.

'What on *earth* is going on?' Mrs Fitzgerald said quietly, in a voice which made Jess's blood run cold.

Claire recovered herself more quickly. 'Jess

came barging into my room and started fighting me,' she said self-righteously. 'You know she's not meant to come in without permission and she didn't even knock. Look, she's broken my lamp!' And she picked up a piece of shattered china, the picture of aggrieved innocence.

'That's not fair—' Jess began, but she knew it was too late.

'Jess – out of Claire's room at once!' her mother snapped. 'I will not tolerate you losing your temper like this. No pocket money for the next month, and you're grounded for the whole weekend.'

'But, Mum – it's the roadshow on Sunday!' Jess protested, horrified. 'Have you forgotten? You can't make me miss that! I've got a ticket and everything!'

'I *can* make you miss it and I will,' Mrs Fitzgerald replied icily. 'Maybe a punishment that really means something will teach you a lesson. And I'm sure one of your friends could use a spare ticket.'

Even Claire had the grace to look taken aback, and Jess felt her eyes begin to prickle with tears.

This was a disaster! She'd been looking forward to the roadshow for ever! Surely her mum didn't seriously mean to keep her locked away at home while everyone else had the time of their lives?

But one look at Mrs Fitzgerald's angry, determined face told Jess that was exactly what she *did* mean to do.

Even if Jess's spaghetti bolognaise had been the most delicious dish in the world – which she had to admit it wasn't – she couldn't have forced herself to eat very much at supper that evening. It was an awkward meal, and she escaped to her bedroom as soon as she could. Let Claire help with the washing-up! If she'd done what she was meant to in the first place, none of this would have happened. She lay on the bed upstairs, gazing at her StarStruck posters and feeling sorry for herself.

She must have fallen asleep because the sound of someone knocking on the bedroom door startled her awake into darkness. 'Phone for you, Jess,' Eddie was calling.

It was Michelle, ringing up to see if she was going to come shopping the next day.

'Miche, I've been grounded!' Jess told her. 'I can't go shopping and I can't go to the roadshow either!'

'What?' Michelle sounded appalled. 'But that's terrible! What did you do?'

'I had a fight with Claire,' Jess said miserably. 'It was all her fault, the stupid . . .' She couldn't find the words to describe how she felt about Claire at the moment. 'Anyway, she's got away with it, as usual, but I've been grounded for the whole weekend *and* no pocket money for the next month. It's so unfair!'

'You're telling me!' Michelle agreed. 'D'you think your mum will change her mind? And what's going to happen about your ticket?'

'Mum says I have to try and get somebody else to buy it from me, or ask you to take it back on Sunday so they can sell it on the door,' Jess said.

'I'm sure we won't have to do that,' Michelle reassured her. 'Leanne's a real StarStruck fan – she'd buy your ticket, no problem. You might even make a profit!'

'But, Miche, I don't want to sell it in the first

place!' Jess wailed. 'We can't give up, just like that! Don't you want me to come?'

'Oh, of course I do,' Michelle replied guiltily. 'I was only trying to be practical. Look, d'you think your mum would let you have visitors? I'll tell the others what's happened and maybe we can work something out together.'

'She'd better.' Jess was beginning to fight back now. 'I've only been grounded, haven't I? Not put in solitary confinement.'

By the time they'd said goodbye and Jess had hung up, she was feeling slightly better. Tomorrow was another day! She'd probably be able to think up some way of making her mum see how unfair this punishment was. But then she remembered the expression on her mother's face, and sighed. It wasn't going to be easy.

The next morning, Jess woke up early. She lay in bed for a while, going over everything that had happened the day before and wondering how to shape her strategy. Maybe if she brought her mother breakfast in bed and then tried some sweet talking? No, that was too obvious. She decided to spend some quality time with the rats while she thought things over.

The sixth member of their gang, Nikki, had gone to live in California for a while the year before, and Jess was looking after her two pet rats. Frankie and Fred were great – really clever and fun to play with. She let Fred wriggle up her pyjama sleeve and come down the other side. Her parents were talking in the kitchen, but nobody else was up yet; now would be a good time to tackle her mother. Perhaps if she offered to buy Claire a new lamp with her pocket money? When she started getting pocket money again, of course . . .

She tucked Fred in her dressing-gown pocket, put on a sorry expression and sidled into the kitchen to see what her mother thought about this brilliant idea.

'Look, Jess, I know it seems hard,' Mrs Fitzgerald sighed, 'but I have to do something to stop you and Claire fighting like this. It's making all our lives miserable! One way or another, you have to learn to get on with each other. In the meantime, the punishment stands. You're still grounded, I'm afraid.'

Jess could tell when her mother's mind was made up. Without bothering to argue – for the moment, anyway – she went to put Fred back in the cage. Then she vented some of her feelings in a long e-mail to Nikki, telling her how unfair life was and how much she detested her vile older sister. By that time, the kitchen was clear so she was able to demolish several bowls of cereal in peace and quiet, and wander back upstairs to get dressed. But dressed for what? Hanging round the house, that was all. She chose her sloppiest pair of jeans and a faded T-shirt, in protest.

Gradually the house swung into its usual Saturday routine. Mr and Mrs Fitzgerald went to the supermarket, Matt set off for football in the park, Claire rang a friend and arranged to go shopping that afternoon (all right for her, wasn't it?), and Eddie carried on sleeping in his loft room. The morning seemed to be stretching on for ever. Just when Jess thought she was going to drop dead with boredom, hunger and bad temper, she heard a strange noise at her bedroom window. A scratchy, rattling noise. Jumping up to investigate, she discovered that handfuls of gravel were being chucked against the glass – and that Michelle, Caz, Lauren and Sunny were standing in the front garden below.

'Rapunzel, Rapunzel, let down your hair!' Michelle called, flinging her arms wide with a carrier bag in each hand.

'We've come to cheer you up,' Caz said, and Lauren added anxiously, 'D'you think your mum will let us in?'

'She's out doing the shopping,' Jess told them. 'Stay right there and I'll be down in one second!' Bounding down the stairs two at a time, she threw open the front door to let her friends pile in. Boy, was it good to see them!

'I've brought my cowboy hat to show you,' Michelle said, when they were all settled upstairs in Jess's room. 'Look, don't you think it's cool?' She jammed it on her head, danced over to the mirror and went on, 'I'm going to wash my hair tonight and put it in loads of little plaits so it's all wavy for Sunday.'

'Never mind about that,' Sunny said impatiently, crunching herself comfortable in a beanbag on the floor. 'We're meant to be working out how to get Jess un-grounded, aren't we?'

'Thanks, guys,' Jess said gratefully. 'I was beginning to think you'd forgotten about me.'

'As if!' Caz said, giving her a hug.

'Have you tried to reason with your mum?' Lauren asked.

Jess was in the middle of telling them about

her unsuccessful attempts so far when Eddie wandered past, on his way down from the loft in search of breakfast (though it was nearly lunchtime by now). 'What's this?' he smiled, seeing all five girls sprawled out in Jess's room. 'A council of war?'

Eddie obviously knew all about the fight, and he had an interesting take on it. 'If you ask me, Claire's probably feeling guilty,' he told Jess, yawning. 'She's not completely horrible, whatever you might think, and I bet she didn't mean things to go this far. You might be able to get her on your side.'

'But I hate her!' Jess protested. 'I can't bear to look at her, let alone speak to her!'

'You still don't get it, do you?' Eddie rubbed his bleary eyes. 'That's what Mum's going on about! She'll only change her mind if she sees that you and Claire are trying to get along. It's your one chance. Depends how much you want to go to the roadshow, I suppose.' And with that, he ambled off towards the next flight of stairs.

'Your brother is lush,' Michelle sighed, watching Eddie's retreating back.

Jess didn't bother to reply; she was too busy pondering Eddie's advice. In her heart of hearts, she knew he was right. More than any number of breakfasts in bed, or tidy rooms, or new lamps, what her mum really wanted was for Jess and Claire to act differently towards each other. Make an effort to be friends, even. But could Jess possibly manage that? It would have to be the hardest thing she'd ever done. And what if Eddie was wrong and Claire didn't feel guilty at all? Then she'd be doing all that crawling for nothing, and her sister would have won again.

Lauren was obviously thinking along the same lines. 'You'd have to swallow your pride,' she said. 'D'you think you could do it?'

'I don't know.' Jess really wasn't sure. 'And the thing is, why should Claire help me go to the roadshow anyway? I bet she's secretly dead chuffed I've been grounded – no matter what Ed says.'

'There has to be something in it for her,' Sunny said slowly. 'Wasn't there some band she wanted to see? Maybe you could try and get their autograph for her.'

Jess stared at Sunny for a few seconds, and then her face broke into a beaming grin. 'Sunny, you've cracked it! That is the most fantastic idea in the history of the world! Claire's friend Sophie's always going on about this signed poster she  won in a magazine competition. I could try and get a Legendary Dogz one for her! And then she'd have a reason to persuade Mum to let me go. Brilliant!'

'But she was so mean to you!' Michelle said. 'How could you bear to do anything for her? She'll think she can treat you like dirt and get away with it.'

'I know, I know.' Jess winced at the thought of what she had to do. 'But if it's the only way I'll get to the roadshow, then it's worth a try.'

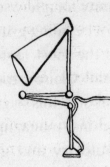

'Wish me luck,' Jess said to the others, grasping her reading lamp. Sunny had suggested she should take this with her as a reason for entering the dragon's lair (i.e. Claire's bedroom) and then use it for bartering once she was inside. She walked slowly along the landing, trying to psyche herself up into the right frame of mind. If Claire thought she was crawling up to apologise, she'd only despise her for being weak. But Jess couldn't risk starting another argument, either; that would only make things ten times worse.

She tapped on her sister's bedroom door and waited to be allowed in.

Claire was standing in front of the full-length mirror, obviously deciding what to wear for her shopping trip. Shoes littered the floor, crumpled

jeans and tops lay on the bed, and she was half in and half out of a white T-shirt. When the mirror revealed Jess standing in the doorway behind her, she hastily wriggled on the empty sleeve. 'Yes? What do you want?'

'I thought you might like to borrow my lamp,' Jess said, holding it out. 'You know, because yours got broken.'

'Oh, right.' Claire looked surprised. 'Yeah, I would. Don't you need it, though?'

'It's OK, I can manage,' Jess replied with a shrug. Claire took the lamp from her – there was an awkward moment when their fingers touched for a second – and plugged it in on her bedside table.

'Look, I've had an idea about the roadshow,' Jess went on, steeling herself. 'I know you really wanted to see Legendary Dogz—'

'Are you trying to sell me your ticket?' Claire said, zipping up her fleece and considering her reflection in the mirror. She'd scraped her mousy hair back into a pony tail, which Jess thought was a mistake. 'I already thought about offering you ten quid for it. But that would mean I'd have to sit with all your creepy friends, so no thanks.'

'That's not exactly what I meant,' Jess said carefully, trying to keep her temper. 'You know Sophie's signed poster? Well, if I went to the roadshow I could get you one too. There's always a chance to queue up for autographs, isn't there? Maybe I could get the lead singer to sign it for you! What's his name – Mungo, Marco, or something?'

'Murdo,' Claire replied, fiddling with her hair. 'But d'you mind me asking how you intend getting to the roadshow? You're grounded, remember?'

This was it: crunch time. 'If we talked to Mum together and you backed me up, I'm sure she'd change her mind,' Jess said. 'Come on, Claire – say you will! You've got to admit, it's not fair me being the only one to get punished for what happened yesterday.'

'Oh, right!' Claire protested. 'You come barging into my room, start fighting and break my lamp—'

'But I was doing all the work on my own!' Jess hit back. 'We were meant to be making supper *together*.' She swallowed hard – no point in opening old wounds – and cast around for something else to persuade Claire. Suddenly, in a blinding flash, it came to her. 'Besides, if Mum saw that you and I were getting on better, think of all the extra brownie points for you! You could even make out it that was your idea to come and see her. I wouldn't mind, honest.'

This was a master stroke! If Claire could act like the leader, she would save face in front of Jess as well as getting the credit for being a peacemaker.

Claire stared at her through narrowed eyes for a few seconds. And then finally she decided. 'OK, I'll do it. We'll tackle her when she's back from the supermarket. But I'm the one doing the talking, understand? Don't start trying to put the boot in about me to Mum. And I want a signed poster – I'll give you some money in case you have to pay for it – *and* I'm keeping the lamp for as long as I like. Deal?'

'Deal,' Jess agreed, and they shook hands.

'And now you can go,' Claire said, turning back to the mirror.

But Jess was already halfway out of the door. She couldn't wait to tell the others that the first part of the plan had worked, and then hustle them back to Michelle's before her parents came home. If she and Claire worked on their mum together, they were bound to succeed. She could see herself at the roadshow already!

### Phone call – Saturday afternoon

**Jess**: At last! I thought you were never going to pick up the phone.

**Michelle**: Give me a chance. We've been taking everyone home – I've only just come through the door.

**Jess**: So, don't you want to know what happened?

**Michelle**: Er, no.

**Jess**: Ha ha, very funny. Well, I'm telling you anyway. We did it! Mum says I can go to the roadshow tomorrow after all. Isn't that fantastic?

**Michelle**: Great! I knew you would. But what did Claire actually say?

**Jess**: You should have heard her! I nearly threw up. She did this whole number about realising the effect our arguments must be having on the rest of the family, and even though I was always the one who started them—

**Michelle**: Charming!

**Jess**: I know! I had to bite my lip a few times, I can tell you. Where was I? Oh yeah, even though I always started them, she could have tried harder to ignore me. Can you imagine?

**Michelle**: I'd have killed her!

**Jess**: I felt like it. But then she did tell Mum that she hadn't helped me much last night – *much*! – and admitted it really wasn't fair I should be taking all the blame. So Mum said that as we'd shown we could cooperate, and as perhaps she had been a bit too harsh, she was prepared to think again about grounding me. I still miss next month's pocket money, though. And Claire gets away without being punished at all – as usual.

**Michelle**: Typical! The jammy—!

**Jess**: Just what I thought. Anyway, is your mum still OK about taking us over to Caz's?

**Michelle**: Course she is. Can you come round here about ten? Don't be late, will you?
**Jess**: Are you kidding? I'll see you for breakfast!

'Turn up the volume!' Jess shouted, bursting into Caz's living room with Michelle the next morning. 'This is the best song ever!'

StarStruck's latest single, 'Second Time Around', was blasting out of the sound system, and Lauren, Sunny and Caz were dancing in time. (Well, almost.) The party had begun!

'You haven't got that move right,' Michelle yelled above the music, wading in to show Caz how it should be done. 'You have to make a square shape with your arms at the side of your head, like this.' And she demonstrated. 'Link your fingers and put your hands at the side of your left cheek, so your head's kind of tucked into your elbow. Got it? Then on the next beat, you switch arms to the right. It's a classic locking move.'

Michelle went to drama classes every Saturday, where she learned how to dance and sing as well as act, so she considered herself quite an expert. She was the best mover out of all of them, it had to be said, and she had a fantastic voice too. Life just isn't fair, Jess thought, trying to copy Michelle as she swung effortlessly into the next part of the routine.

Michelle suddenly stopped abruptly. 'Maybe I should have worn jeans and trainers,' she fretted. 'This dress is too tight to dance properly.'

'But it looks great,' Lauren said. 'And your hat is wicked!' The sparkly pink stetson did look fantastic with Michelle's denim dress.

Jess was feeling good about her own outfit, too – she loved her black flares, which she'd teamed with a T-shirt that had 'Diva' picked out in sequins on the front. Lauren looked more of a hippy chick, in her beaded T-shirt and a pair of low-slung jeans with velvet ribbon, braid and 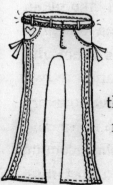sequins running up the seams. She'd worn them with a glittery belt, buckled at the back – the perfect finishing touch. Lauren was the artistic one in the group, forever ripping her clothes apart and putting them back together in some amazingly creative way.

Sunny had gone for the hippy look too, wearing one of the muslin shirts she'd brought back from her last trip to India with a big embroidered bag slung over one shoulder which she refused to put down in case she left it behind. Being dead practical, she'd probably brought loads of useful things along, like a water bottle and something to read.

Lastly, Caz was wearing baggy combats and a logo T-shirt like Jess's – 'Wild Thing' – with a funky bandanna tied over her hair. She spends far too much time worrying about other people's feelings to be really wild, Jess thought to herself, and smiled. Caz was a sweetie, and it was mainly because of her that they were going to the road-show at all. She'd organised everything: persuading her stepsister Natalie to take them, sending off for tickets, and working out how they were going to get there. Caz's mum and stepdad were taking them to the station in two cars, and then they'd be going to the arena by train.

Natalie's new boyfriend, Josh, was coming too. Caz was the only one who'd met him, and she'd reported that he was a Goth like her stepsister – all black clothes, dead white skin and spiky dark hair. Still, Natalie might look weird but she was really nice underneath, so maybe Josh would turn out to be the same. And they didn't have to stick with the happy couple all the time, did they?

Jess flopped down on the sofa, her eyes sparkling. 'This roadshow's going to be so great!' she declared, leaning back into the cushions. 'Can you imagine if Mum had really made me miss it?'

She couldn't help shuddering at the thought. It had been a narrow escape.

'I didn't realise it was going to be such a pack-out!' Lauren said, looking down a wide central staircase at the thousands of people thronging the entrance halls below.

'Are you OK?' Jess asked, squeezing her hand. They all knew that Lauren felt jumpy in the middle of large crowds; she liked to make sure she could leave quickly, in case of emergencies. 'Do you want me to come outside with you for some fresh air?'

'No, thanks, I'm all right at the moment,' Lauren replied, linking arms with Jess. 'This is great, isn't it?'

'Amazing!' she agreed, a big smile on her face. The atmosphere had been building up ever since they'd filed off the train, pushed their way along the busy platform and joined a river of fans streaming towards the arena. Traders had set up stalls around the entrance selling flags, posters, T-shirts and whistles, and a couple of men were walking up and down with bundles of glow-sticks and tinsel 'ears' slung over their arms. Jess had thought about buying a StarStruck flag, but decided they looked rather tacky. She wished she'd thought to bring a home-made one, like the group of girls carrying a huge Highway 101 banner with 'Blow us a kiss!' written on the other side. Anyway, she'd managed to find a great Legendary Dogz poster for Claire – there'd be time enough later to think about getting it signed.

Now the girls were inside, where a buzz of excitement crackled in the air like electricity. Shrill whistle blasts sounded from all sides, and everyone seemed to be talking and laughing, or calling to their friends as they wandered from one event to another. The auditorium itself wasn't open yet, but there were loads of things to watch or take part in all around it. Jess, Lauren, Caz, Sunny and Michelle were queuing up for a turn in the karaoke area: a roped-off temporary platform with spotlights above it and a huge sound system in one corner. A DJ – whose face Jess vaguely recognised from Saturday-morning television – was encouraging people to sing along to backing music, while screens overhead showed the real pop stars performing.

'This lot are hopeless,' Michelle said scathingly, watching the girls who were strutting their stuff on stage. 'They don't know the words and they're not bothering to dance either. We're like, a million times better than them.'

'Come on, it's only a laugh,' Caz told her, waving at Natalie and Josh, who were waiting in the audience. 'Anyway, *we* might not get a song we know when it's our turn.'

'I'm so nervous,' Sunny said, hopping around from one foot to the other. 'Look at all those people who'll be watching us!'

But there was no time to back out – the music faded away, the dreary girls shuffled offstage, and before Sunny could pretend she needed the loo, the others had dragged her off with them towards the waiting microphones. They were in luck: now the video screens changed to show the boys from Highway 101 (to a huge cheer from the audience), and the opening notes of 'Waking Dreams' came blasting out.

'Brilliant!' Michelle said, adjusting her stetson before she bounded on stage. 'Now let's knock 'em dead.'

'And who have we got here?' the DJ asked, smiling at them. 'I didn't think Madonna could make it today. D'you know this track, girls?'

'Sure. It's one of our favourites.' Michelle spoke for all of them.

'Not mine!' Jess muttered, but her words were lost under more screams from the audience. Most people seemed to agree with Michelle's view of the band, rather than hers. 'OK, then, Madonna – here we go!' the DJ said, without wasting any more time.

Michelle didn't need asking twice: her powerful voice soared into the first verse of the song, and the others joined in more quietly alongside. Jess in particular kept the volume down – knowing her limitations – but she worked out a cool kind of shuffle while the others sang. A few steps to the side, swivel around and lean your shoulders back, then bend your knees with your hands on your hips. Soon Lauren and Caz had picked it up, and Jess felt as though she would burst with pride; they looked so professional! People in the audience were whistling and cheering some more, and burst into a deafening round of applause when the song finally finished.

'That was great,' the DJ said, sounding like he really meant it. 'You lot can come back any time.'

After that amazing experience, they were all on too much of a high to think straight, so Natalie suggested going to the café for a drink and the chance to wind down before deciding what to do next.

'I saw those guys with the camera filming you,' Josh said casually, pointing to a couple of men threading their way through the crush. One had a camera on his shoulder with an overhead microphone and lights, and the other was using a hand-held mike to interview fans in the crowd.

Michelle nearly choked on her Coke. 'Really? When we were singing? What for? Are we going to be on TV? Oh, wow – that is so incredible!'

'Calm down,' Natalie said, laughing. 'They might play some of what they've shot before the show starts, that's all.'

'That's *all*?' Caz repeated, her voice rising with excitement. 'We might be up on some huge screen in front of thousands of people and you're saying it's no big deal? Nat, don't you realise this is just about the most exciting thing that's ever happened to us?'

'OK, OK. I get the message,' Natalie said, raising her hands in surrender. 'So what do you pop idols want to try next? There's about an hour till the main event.'

'We have to go for the dance auditions,' Michelle said decisively. 'If we carry on like this, how can we possibly lose? They're bound to pick us.'

Lauren and Caz wanted to dance too, but Sunny hadn't forgotten about the chance to try out as a pop presenter. 'I've written down loads of good questions to ask,' she said, taking a notebook out of her embroidered bag and flicking over the pages.

'I'll come with you,' Jess offered. Seeing herself on film sounded more appealing than trying to follow some complicated dance routine. Making up her own moves or copying steps from the TV on her own was one thing. Following instructions from a professional instructor in the middle of a big group – in public! – was another. She was bound to fall over her feet.

'Is it OK if we split up?' Lauren asked Natalie. 'There isn't time for us all to do both, is there?'

'As long as you two stick together,' Natalie told Sunny and Jess. 'You can meet us over by the dance studio in half an hour or so. OK? Or do you think maybe Josh should come with you?'

'Oh, don't worry!' Jess said hastily. 'We'll be fine.' She could tell that Josh felt the roadshow wasn't really his thing – he kept looking around as if he were afraid of bumping into somebody he knew. Besides, he wasn't exactly chatty, and she had no idea what to say to him. They'd be much better off on their own.

'I'll give you your tickets,' Natalie said, taking them out of her bag. 'If you're late for any reason, come straight into the auditorium. And stick together, remember!'

Sunny and Jess made their way over to a far corner of one of the halls, where they'd spotted a sign saying 'Junior Journalist'. A queue of would-be interviewers were standing in a line leading up to a squashy sofa with lights all around it and a camera in front.

Sunny watched the action for a few minutes. 'That girl on the sofa's pretending to be some new pop star,' she said, nudging Jess. 'And the boy with glasses must be the one who's interviewing her. See? You can watch it all on this monitor here. Looks like a real TV programme, doesn't it?'

'Mmm,' Jess answered absent-mindedly. She was busy ear-wigging on the conversation behind them. A couple of girls who'd just joined the queue were talking about a back entrance to the hall where you could wait for the stars' autographs. They sounded quite friendly, so she turned round to ask them exactly where it was.

'You have to go out of the main doors and turn left down the side, then left again just before the car park,' one of the girls said. 'That takes you to the back entrance which all the acts use – like a stage door. Remember to take your ticket so you can get back in again.'

'Somebody said Rick from Highway 101 was going to come out,' her friend added. 'But we were hanging around there for hours and he didn't show, so we've given up.'

'You didn't see anyone from Legendary Dogz, did you?' Jess asked hopefully.

'No way! We'd have run a mile if we had,' the first girl said, giggling.

Jess took her point, but she had promised Claire she'd try and get a signed poster – she ought to make an effort. 'Can you save my place?' she asked Sunny. 'I'm just nipping out for a while. Won't be long, I promise.'

'But Natalie said we had to stick together!' Sunny protested. 'Where are you going? What if you get lost?'

'I'll come straight back,' Jess said, 'and I've got my ticket anyway. Relax, Sunny! Nothing's going to go wrong.'

With that, she was off, threading her way through the crowds towards the arena's main entrance. It felt quite exciting, doing something on her own for once. Of course she loved being in the middle of a gang of friends, but it was great to be independent sometimes too. No one else to worry about – she could go where she wanted, do as she pleased.

Clutching the poster in one hand and her ticket in the other, she slipped out into the street and down a side road towards the car park. There was the second left turning, and as she rounded the corner she saw a crowd of girls waiting by a gate in the railings at the back of the arena. They all looked much older than Jess, and her confidence began to ebb away as she walked up to join them. She stuck her hands in her pockets and leaned against the railings at the edge of the group, trying to look casual.

Ten minutes later, precisely nothing had happened. No one had come out of the doorway they were all watching so intently, and Jess was fed up. She caught the eye of a girl in leather trousers who was standing nearest to her. 'This is a drag, isn't it?' she said, trying to strike up a conversation. 'I'm trying to get a Legendary Dogz autograph. For my sister, not me – they're not really my scene.'

'You've just missed him,' the girl replied. She blew a large pink bubble out of gum, then snapped it matter-of-factly with her tongue and stuffed the gum back in her mouth. 'The lead singer, that is. He came out here a little while ago, but nobody was that bothered so he went back inside. We're all waiting for Highway 101.'

'Oh, right,' Jess said. 'Thanks.' So that was that – no point in hanging around any longer. Still, at least she could tell Claire that she'd tried.

Keen to get back to the action and put Sunny's mind at rest, Jess set off quickly towards the arena. A guard wearing a black jacket with 'Security' on the back in reflecting silver letters was also hurrying in the same direction, just ahead of her on the other side of the railings. He must be going to check things out backstage, she thought to herself. Wonder what it's like in there? She could imagine the bands waiting to go out and perform – feeling nervous, maybe, as they ran through their numbers.

She could see the guard quite clearly now through a gap in the railings up ahead. He reached the back of the building, paused at a side door for a few seconds and then disappeared inside, leaving the door swinging behind him. And suddenly, without really thinking what she was doing, Jess decided to follow. Why shouldn't she see what was happening behind the scenes for herself? Who could tell – she might even bump into StarStruck somewhere backstage. A chance meeting like that was worth risking anything for!

In the space of a few of seconds, she'd

squeezed through the gap in the railings, sprinted across a few metres of tarmac and made it safely to the door. Quickly she pushed it wide open, glancing back over her shoulder at the crowd of girls still hanging around on the other side of the gate. Ha, more fool them! She'd spotted her chance and seized it with both hands. Sometimes direct action was needed if you wanted to make things happen!

6

access all areas

Closing the door quietly behind her, Jess was confronted by a long corridor stretching away into the distance. She could see the guard up ahead: the silver 'Security' lettering on his jacket shone out in the gloom. As stealthily as possible, she set off behind, hoping the passage would branch into a larger space in which she could lose herself. Now that she was inside the building – where she had no right to be – it was hard to feel quite so brave. The corridor was dimly lit by a couple of bare lightbulbs, and silent except for the sound of the man's footsteps and her own as she padded after him.

He turned a corner at the end of the corridor. Ten seconds later, Jess turned it too – and then gasped in shock. A hand had snaked out of nowhere to grab her by a handful of T-shirt, and a stubbly, bad-tempered face was pressed up against hers. The guard had lain in wait for her around the corner.

'You're following me, aren't you?' he growled. 'Why? What are you doing here? Do you have a path?'

What? Jess didn't have a clue what he was going on about. Was there some kind of route she should be following? She couldn't think straight: her heart was beating so hard she thought it would leap out of her chest. 'I d-don't know what you mean,' she stammered, recoiling in fear. 'I'm sorry! Please let me go. I'm not doing anything wrong, honestly!'

'Thith ith a rethtricted area,' the man said, glaring at her. Then he thrust a kind of clip-on badge under Jess's nose. 'Show me your path!'

Now Jess understood: the man had a lisp, and he was asking to see her pass. Which of course she didn't have. 'I'm sorry,' she said, spreading her hands wide. 'I've – I've – left it behind somewhere. Please, if you let me go I'll fetch it straight away.' Desperately, she tried to think up some excuse to get her off the hook. 'I'm here with my mum – she works in the kitchens – and I wandered off and got lost.'

She was really scared by now. There was nobody else around and the guard looked so menacing! He wasn't particularly tall or well-built, but something about his expression would convince the toughest trouble-maker that he meant business. He had thin, mean-looking lips set in a bony face, and a shock of dark greasy hair. Jess had no idea what he was going to do next.

He stared at her suspiciously for a few seconds. Then, seeming to make up his mind, he started to haul her back the way they'd come – still keeping a tight hold on her T-shirt. 'Thtupid girl,' she could hear him muttering under his breath. 'Wathting my time.' He was obviously still in a hurry: she had to half-run along beside him to keep up as he hustled her back to the exit. When they reached it, he simply opened the door and pushed her out. This time, he made sure it was properly shut; Jess heard the lock click into place.

She stood there, blinking in the open air, while

a mixture of emotions flooded through her. Relief, because she was safely outside; embarrassment, because she should never have tried such a crazy thing in the first place; and then indignation, because the guard didn't have to be quite so unpleasant, did he? She was a fan, not a criminal. If he'd asked her nicely she'd have left straight away, without having to be dragged along beside him like this.

Oh, well. She smoothed down her T-shirt, looked around to check whether anyone had been watching (luckily they hadn't), and then set off back to find Sunny with as much dignity as she could muster. She wasn't going to let some bully spoil her day!

'At last! I've been going out of my head! Where on earth have you been?' Sunny was frantic by the time Jess joined her again under the Junior Journalist sign.

'I'm sorry,' she said, waving her Legendary Dogz poster in its (now rather tatty) carrier bag. 'I kept thinking one of them was going to come out any second and nobody ever did.' She'd decided to keep her little adventure to herself – there was no need for the others to know about it. 'What's been going on here? Where's everybody gone?'

'They've turned away all the people behind me because the interviews have to finish,' Sunny told her. 'I've told them I'm saving a place for you, but you might be too late. Hang on – I think it's my turn now! Watch me on the monitor, won't you?'

'Sure,' Jess said, patting Sunny on the back as she set off for the comfy sofa. 'Good luck!'

Sunny *had* thought up some interesting questions to ask the (pretend) pop star, but she didn't come across very well on film. Her voice sounded quite soft and shy, and she kept her head down while she was speaking so the girl she was interviewing found it difficult to hear her. Jess decided to try and make more of an impact when it was her turn.

'Right. Is that it?' the cameraman said, looking round as Sunny's session drew to a close.

'I'm next!' Jess called, jumping up and down

and waving to get his attention. 'Please! I'm her friend and we've been waiting for ages!' (Which was almost true.) 'Please let me have a go!'

'Oh, all right,' the cameraman sighed. 'But you are absolutely the last person, OK? Otherwise we're not going to have time to look at all the clips.'

'How did I do?' Sunny whispered to Jess as they changed places. She gave her the thumbs-up in reply and whispered back, 'Great!'

'Hi, there. My name's Amelia, and I want you to imagine that I've just released a single that's gone straight into the top ten,' the girl on the sofa said to Jess. She stifled a yawn. 'Oh, excuse me. Now, who are you? And what would you like to ask me?'

I bet she's dead bored, saying the same thing over and over again, Jess thought. She decided to try and wake Amelia up a bit – even make her laugh if she could. 'I'm Jess Fitzgerald, your number one fan,' she began. 'And I've just seen your video. It's no wonder you're tired! Where did you learn to dance like that?'

With that, they were away. Amelia smiled and

made up some answer about her imaginary video which gave Jess an idea for her next question. Soon, between them they'd invented a glittering career for Amelia: her chart-topping latest album, the forthcoming world tour and soon-to-be filmed life story. It all seemed so real that Jess almost began to believe she really *was* a pop star.

'What's it like,' she asked, perching on the edge of the sofa, 'when you're standing out there on stage in front of thousands of people? Are you nervous?'

Amelia laughed and stretched out her arms. 'I'm sorry,' she said. 'I'm sure you could carry on for ages, but we really do have to stop now. Thanks, Jess – that was great. I hope you win!'

'Win what?' Jess asked Sunny when they were together again. 'Is there some kind of prize?'

'Of course there is!' Sunny couldn't believe her ears. 'Jessie, you airhead, that's the whole point! Don't you remember me telling you? The person they think is best has the chance to go backstage and do an interview for real. What else did you think it was for?'

Jess shrugged. 'I dunno. To see yourself on film, I suppose.' If only she'd realised this Junior Journalist thing was a competition! She'd have tried so much harder. 'Well, I've blown my chances there. Come on, let's see if Michelle's won the dance audition.'

'I can see Caz!' Sunny said, clutching Jess's arm as they approached the side room where the auditions were being held. 'Look, she's there in the front row. But where's Michelle? And Lauren?'

'There they are! Sitting at the side, with Natalie and Josh,' Jess reported. 'Oh, dear. Michelle doesn't look very happy.'

That was an understatement. Michelle was sitting on the bench with a face like thunder, and they soon discovered why. She hadn't even made it through the first round of auditions.

'It's *so* unfair,' she grumbled to Sunny and Jess. 'Just because I was wearing the wrong thing! I knew this dress was going to be too tight. And look at some of the people she's picked! That girl in the orange T-shirt couldn't keep in time to save her life!'

There were about thirty girls – and four brave boys – on the floor, being taught a dance routine by a dynamic instructor in leggings with a microphone on a headset.

'This is the final group,' Lauren told them. 'Caz has done really well to get this far! The teacher taps you on the shoulder at the end if she wants you to stay for the next round.'

Jess was glad she'd decided to opt for the interview session. She'd never have mastered all the steps in this dance sequence: forward on the right foot, three steps, bounce around to the left, two steps together, click your fingers, elbows out and p-u-s-h forward. Then bend one knee and spring back – no wonder Michelle couldn't manage in her denim dress.

She waved at Caz to give her some moral support. Caz managed a quick wave in return, but unfortunately, things went downhill from then on. She lost the beat, stepped the wrong way coming out of her bounce, and collided with the girl next to her. Then she caught Lauren's eye and started giggling, so that was that. Total meltdown. It came as no surprise to anyone, least of all Caz, that she wasn't part of the final winning group. When the session was over, she staggered back to join her friends on the bench.

'Well done!' they chorused, crowding round to congratulate her. 'That was fantastic!'

'But I was so bad at the end,' Caz said, wiping tears of laughter from her eyes. 'I couldn't do a thing! Still, I really enjoyed it. Sorry you didn't get through, guys.'

'Oh, that's OK. I thought you were great,' Michelle said generously. Seeing Caz mess up seemed to have put her in a better mood. 'Anyway, these auditions are only for fun, aren't they?'

'We might as well go and find our seats,' Natalie said, looking at her watch. 'We've done everything we want to do here, haven't we? Let's check out the auditorium.'

They made their way to the entrance gate printed on their tickets (Jess had a major panic thinking she'd lost hers until she found it safe in a back pocket) along several passages and finally into the main arena. There must have been at least a thousand people already in their places among the towering banks of seats. A steward helped Natalie find out where they were sitting: in the front section, up one level on the left-hand side.

'Hey, these seats are great,' Caz said, settling herself down between Michelle and Natalie, who was sitting with Josh at the end of the row. 'What a fantastic view!'

'And look at those massive screens.' Sunny pointed them out: two on either side of the stage. Some pop videos were currently playing, featuring the bands who were going to be appearing later. Highway 101 seemed to be the favourites: they got by far the loudest cheers and whistle blasts from the audience. Jess yelled her heart out whenever StarStruck were shown, to even out the balance, and there were some fans in the row behind her who joined in too.

She took a mouthful of the candyfloss she'd just bought and felt its sticky sweetness dissolve on her tongue. There was such a great vibe in the air – everyone enjoying themselves but holding something back until the bands appeared. When StarStruck come on stage, I'm going to go crazy, Jess told herself happily. She couldn't wait!

After what seemed like an age, the video screens went blank, lights began to dim around the auditorium, and coloured spotlights focused on the stage. The set had been designed to look like a giant-sized recording studio, with sound booths, microphones and huge jukeboxes. Clouds of silver helium balloons tied on strings bobbed gently in the air.

Jess nudged Lauren in the seat next to her. 'I think it's starting – at last!'

No sooner were the words out of her mouth than a van backed on to the stage and three DJs burst out of the back, to a roar from the audience. This time Jess definitely recognised them: she watched the two guys and a girl on TV every Saturday morning. She couldn't remember the guys' names, but the girl was called Frankie and she was really fun. All three of them knew just how to whip up the crowd – soon everyone was shouting, blowing shrill whistle blasts and drumming their feet on the floor. Even Josh had started to look like he was enjoying himself. It was a riot!

'OK, calm down for a second,' Frankie told everyone eventually. 'We're going to play some of the clips we shot earlier, so take a good look at the video screens. You and your friends might be up there!'

'And watch out for our camera operators going round the audience,' one of the male DJs added. 'We'll be filming right through the show.'

'Yes!' Michelle clutched Caz's arm. 'This is it: our chance to hit the big time!'

Some of the footage showed people milling around outside the arena, holding banners, blowing whistles – even singing their favourite numbers or starting an impromptu dance routine. There were interviews inside with a group of girls who'd come in a stretch limo for a birthday treat, and a couple of boys who could breakdance. And then, quite out of the blue, there *they* were, on all four screens:

Michelle singing her heart out in a sparkly pink stetson and the others dancing next to her, ten times larger than life.

'That's us!' Lauren screamed, unnecessarily, as they all shrieked with joy and clutched each other.

'Are we cool, or what?' Sunny shouted above the din, and Jess nodded. 'Definitely!' For a couple of seconds, she'd had a glimpse of how they might look as a girl band – and it was great!

But all too soon, the images on screen had changed; in another part of the auditorium, it was somebody else's turn to go wild at the sight of themselves on film. Michelle sighed with satisfaction and dug deep into her carton of popcorn. 'That was amazing,' she said. 'Don't you think my hat looked fantastic?'

The rest of the images passed by in a blur – they were still stunned by their moment of glory. Jess dimly heard one of the DJs say, 'Last but not least, time for one important announcement before the show begins: the result of our Junior

Journalist competition!' but she didn't pay that much attention. She honestly didn't think she had a hope of winning – not having taken the interview half seriously enough – and as far as she could tell, Sunny wasn't a contender either.

So when she saw a clip of herself on screen, chatting away to Amelia, and heard Frankie saying, 'And the winner is – Jess Fitzgerald!' it was so absolutely, utterly amazing that she simply couldn't take it in. It felt as though she'd stepped into some fantasy land where even the wildest dreams could come true. She sat there, opening and shutting her mouth like a fish, while her friends leapt to their feet and went generally crazy all around her.

'Jess! What's the matter with you?' Caz yelled, pulling her up out of the seat. 'You've won! We need to find one of the stewards and tell them who you are. You have to go down on the stage – they're asking for you!'

With that, Jess came to life. Her legs might have turned to jelly, but she couldn't waste time when the biggest adventure of her life was about to begin. And she wasn't going to leave her friends behind, either. 'Let's go!' she said, grabbing Caz's arm and pulling Lauren along too. 'You're coming with me!'

'Do you think we're allowed?' Lauren shouted, stumbling along the row of seats.

'Well, it's worth a try!' Jess replied, grinning from ear to ear. 'What's the matter? Don't you want to go backstage?'

'Are you crazy?' Michelle screamed, already jumping up and down with Sunny in the aisle. 'Try holding us back!'

Jess soon found out the answer to the question she'd asked Amelia. It felt absolutely terrifying, standing on stage in front of thousands of people – but terrifying in a wonderful, thrilling, goosebumps-on-the-skin kind of way. The spotlights were dazzling, and she couldn't see past them into the sea of shadowy faces that made up the audience. She could hear everyone, though: a great wave of sound rose up out of the darkness and crashed over her. She turned back to the wings, where her friends were waiting with Natalie (who'd insisted on coming along too), and gave them a thumbs-up sign. She hoped Sunny wasn't feeling too jealous – she'd so badly wanted to win the competition for herself.

But there wasn't time to worry about that. Frankie had put a reassuring arm round her shoulder and was saying, 'Congratulations, Jess! We want you to go backstage now and do a special interview for us which will be screened on national TV next weekend. Are you up for that?'

Jess nodded. She seemed to have lost the power of speech, though Frankie was waving a microphone hopefully under her nose. She'd better learn to talk again quickly, or the interview would be a washout!

Frankie smiled and gave her shoulder a comforting squeeze. 'Don't worry, you'll be fine,' she whispered off air, before carrying on into the mike, 'And the band we've lined up for you to interview is – wait for it – StarStruck! So what do you think about that, Jess? Are you a fan of theirs?'

'What!' This was too much – Jess thought she was going to pass out. She grabbed the microphone and squeaked into it, 'I am, like, the biggest StarStruck fan in the history of the world!'

Her voice boomed back at top volume, startling her for a second, but she didn't care. She was going to meet her heroes! Actually see them in the flesh and talk to them, face to face – if she didn't die of excitement first. 'They are the best band ever!' she declared, and all the other StarStruck fans in the audience yelled and whistled to show they agreed.

Everything now seemed even more dreamlike than before. Jess was handed over to somebody in a 'Crew' T-shirt called Bill, who would be their guide backstage. He said it was fine for her friends to come along too, as long as they didn't get in the way when the interview was being filmed.

'I don't believe this!' Michelle kept saying. 'Who d'you think we'll meet?' She grabbed Jess's arm in her excitement. 'Hey, maybe we'll see Highway 101! I'm going to pass out, I just know it!'

Jess couldn't stop grinning as she clipped on the 'ACCESS ALL AREAS' security pass they'd each been given. It reminded her briefly of the horrible security guard. He could see her path thith time, no problem! 'So what if we *see* Highway 101?' she told Michelle. 'I'm going to be *talking* to StarStruck! Can you imagine?'

'Let me know if you need any ideas for questions,' Sunny said, and Jess hugged her to show she understood how Sunny might be feeling.

'Just watch your step,' Bill warned as they set off, with a sound engineer and a camera operator who'd be filming the interview. 'There are wires everywhere – mind you don't trip over them.'

It was dark backstage, and there was an atmosphere of – well, not panic, exactly, but chaotic activity. Cables snaked along the ground and technicians swarmed around them, checking connections and gabbling into walkie-talkies. Jess nearly bumped straight into a group of people waiting in the wings, and mumbled her apologies.

'Did you realise who that was?' Caz hissed in her ear. 'You almost crashed into Nomad just then!'

Jess gasped in disbelief. Nomad, the Irish band opening the show, were really famous! She turned back to call out 'Good luck!' to the lead singer, and he waved to her in return.

'You've got a nerve!' Lauren giggled beside her, but Jess didn't care. This was probably the only time she'd ever go backstage, and she was determined to make the most of it!

Now they were walking through an archway and into a warren of corridors with doors on either side, like the one Jess had crept along what now seemed like a lifetime earlier. It felt so good to know that she'd earned the right to be backstage this time.

'These must be the dressing rooms,' Sunny said. 'Look at the signs on the doors!'

Jess couldn't believe that they were only separated from so many amazing celebrities by a thin piece of wood. At any moment, one of the doors might open and somebody dead famous could come out. Here was Nomad's dressing room, and Taneesha's, and Jive Posse, and Eastside – and next to them, Highway 101! The door was slightly ajar and she could hear a burst of laughter from inside. She nudged Michelle and pointed to the sign on the door.

Michelle's eyes widened and she hurried to catch up with Bill, who was walking ahead of them with Natalie. 'Can we stop to get autographs?' she asked breathlessly.

'On the way back, maybe,' he told her. 'We're a bit strapped for time just now.'

A couple of doors further along, the sign read, 'Legendary Dogz', and Jess kicked herself for having left Claire's poster under her seat. Why hadn't she thought to bring it along? And then a small knot of people materialised in the corridor ahead, clustered together in a huddle around another of the dressing-room doors. Two huge men in suits and dark glasses stood one on either side of it. A girl with a clipboard detached herself from the group when she caught sight of Bill and came hurrying towards them.

'Just hang on here for a second,' he told the girls. 'I won't be long.'

'What's the matter?' Jess asked. 'Is there a problem?' But Bill was already walking off and didn't hear – or he pretended not to.

'I hope everything's OK,' Jess said anxiously to her friends. There was something worrying about the expression on everyone's faces and the way they were talking to each other in low, urgent undertones.

After what seemed like an age, Bill came slowly back towards them. 'I'm really sorry,' he began, looking troubled, 'but there's been a slight hitch.'

'What do you mean?' Jess felt her stomach lurch. 'What's happened?'

'Well, I'm afraid we're going to have to call off the interview with StarStruck,' Bill went on, rubbing his forehead. 'I'm sorry – I know how much you were looking forward to it. But I'm afraid their schedule's had to be changed and now there won't be time for them to talk to you.'

Jess stared at him in dismay. This wasn't a slight hitch, it was a major disaster! The most wonderful opportunity had come to her out of the blue, and now it was being cruelly snatched away. She couldn't bear it!

'Don't worry, though,' Bill was saying.

'There's another great band who'd be happy to talk to you. Legendary Dogz! So you can interview them and still be on the kids' channel next weekend. That's OK, isn't it?'

'Legendary Dogz?' Jess repeated faintly.

No, that was most definitely *not* OK! Legendary Dogz were so scary! What kind of questions could she possibly ask them? 'Do you have any interesting hobbies?' 'What's your favourite shop?' They'd probably make her feel really foolish.

'Why don't we go autograph-hunting while you do the interview?' Michelle asked hopefully, but Jess wasn't having any of it.

'No way! I need some moral support,' she told her friends firmly.

Bill was already taking them back down the corridor. He knocked on the door with the Legendary Dogz sign (plus a cute little skull and crossbones underneath) and smiled down at Jess as they waited for a response. 'Don't worry,' he whispered. 'Their bark's worse than their bite.'

Oh yeah? Jess thought. Wanna bet?

'Maybe we should just forget about this.' Jess tugged nervously at Bill's sleeve. 'I don't mind not doing an interview. Really.'

Nobody had come to answer their knock on the dressing-room door and she could hear raised voices coming from inside. It sounded as though there was some huge row going on.

'But we need some footage for Saturday's show,' Bill replied, knocking again. 'And they should be expecting us. Come on, let's go straight in.'

He opened the door without waiting for an invitation and marched in, followed by the film crew – and lastly, tentatively, Natalie, Jess and the others.

After the brightly lit corridor, it was difficult to adjust to the darkness inside Legendary Dogz' dressing room. A single red lightbulb on a lamp in one corner struggled to make an impact, and the place seemed to be full of hulking, indistinct shapes. As Jess's eyes became used to the gloom, she realised that Murdo, the lead singer – whom she recognised from Claire's posters – was standing in the middle of the room, lifting another man almost off the floor by the shoulders of his black leather jacket. Their faces were inches apart and they were hissing insults at each other. She and Lauren exchanged horrified glances. This was not good.

Even Bill seemed rather put out. 'Excuse me, guys,' he said, scandalised. 'We've come for the kids' channel interview. Remember? This is Jess Fitzgerald, our prize-winner, and her friends.'

Murdo swung round and stared at him for a moment. Then he set the man down without another word, pulled out a plastic chair from a nearby table and sat astride it, plonking his booted feet one on either side. 'OK,' he growled in a sandpaper-and-cigarettes Scottish accent. 'Start interviewing. What d'ye want to know?'

Jess felt every drop of confidence she

possessed drain away into a puddle on the floor. This was not going to be like a cosy chat with Amelia! And were the band really suitable for children's television, anyway? They'd give all the little kids nightmares.

'We'll have to do something about the lighting first,' the camera woman said. 'Does anyone mind if I switch on the overhead light? That'll be a start.'

Murdo gave a crazy, barking laugh. 'Aye, go ahead,' he said, waving an arm round the shadowy cave of a room. 'Pu' the light on. Then everyone can see!'

See what? Jess thought. Dead bodies? Wild animals? Nothing would surprise her. She caught Michelle's eye and looked away quickly in case she started giggling.

The overhead light flickered on, revealing a perfectly ordinary-looking room. It might have been rather untidy, with piles of clothes over the floor and the two sofas, but there didn't seem to be anything sinister lurking inside it. Unless you counted the shaven-headed bloke with a studded dog collar round his neck, sitting cross-legged in one corner.

'Hey!' he grumbled, blinking like a startled owl. 'Who turned the light on? Bad karma, man!'

Murdo's knuckles gripped the back of the chair so tightly that the words 'Love' and 'Hate' tattooed on them stood out clearly against his taut skin. 'Look around!' he spat viciously, glaring at the guy he'd been manhandling who was now slumped on one of the sofas. 'Take a look at this room. Ye've turned it into a complete – tip!'

'What?' For a split second, Jess thought she was going to burst out laughing. Murdo sounded just like her mother! And the place wasn't *that* bad, was it? Her bedroom looked much the same.

Murdo jumped up so violently he knocked the chair over. 'How can ah find a thing ta wear,' he stormed, pacing up and down, 'when all oor threads are – on – the – floor?' With each word, he kicked a different heap of clothes, sending them windmilling into the air. Then he stood over the man on the sofa, hands on hips, and snarled, 'When ye've tried something on, hang it back up on the rail. Go' that?'

'Oh, go boil your head,

Murdo. You're crazy,' sofa man said, stretching out his legs and folding his arms. 'Anyway, the stylist'll be here soon.'

'No, she won't,' Murdo replied grimly. 'She's too busy with those wee girlies next door. Ach, ah knew it! We should never ha' agreed to do this gig in the first place.'

'I'll help if you like,' Jess offered, picking a ripped shirt off the floor. 'It's no big deal.' Funnily enough, she felt much less frightened of Murdo now; his anger was so over the top, it was almost funny. She might have a problem controlling her temper but, hey, he was a lot worse!

'Some of these things are really creased,' Lauren said, joining in the tidy-up time. 'Do you have an iron anywhere?'

'Aye, there's one over there,' Murdo said, pointing towards a corner. He sounded a little surprised.

Soon Natalie, Michelle, Sunny and Caz had pitched in too and, even in the space of a few minutes, the place began to look much better. The camera woman set up some extra lights while the sound engineer arranged his mikes and Bill hung around, looking bemused. Legendary Dogz weren't quite sure what to make of it all, either. Jess didn't care. She was sick of standing there with her friends like a lemon – and they were probably missing Nomad's act, too – waiting for this lot to stop arguing. Mind you, after dealing with Claire, she knew how Murdo felt.

'Why don't you try some relaxation exercises?' she told him, searching for a left-footed cowboy boot to match the right one she'd found under a table. 'That's what my mum makes me do when I'm stressed out. You have to breathe deeply and imagine you're on some desert island.'

Michelle interrupted the therapy session, holding up a T-shirt with a snarling tiger's head on it. 'Ooh, this is nice!' she told Murdo, just as though he were one of her mates. 'I bet it would look great with your leather trousers.'

'I'm sorry to interrupt,' Bill said sniffily, obviously deciding that things were getting away from him, 'but we really ought to start filming soon.'

'It's nae use,' Murdo groaned, sinking back into a chair. 'Ah cannae concentrate till we've got oor ootfits sorted. Sorry, gurrls.'

And that's when Jess suddenly had one of her most brilliant ideas ever. 'This interview doesn't have to be straight questions, does it?' she asked Bill. 'What if we did a kind of backstage wardrobe report instead? Maybe I could introduce the band and then we could film them in loads of different clothes, as if they were trying to decide what to wear.'

Bill caught on straight away. 'Yes! I can see exactly what you mean,' he said. 'We could speed up the film, too, and make the whole thing look really comical. It would be a gas. Jess, you're on to something there!'

'And we can help put the outfits together,' Lauren suggested.

'With Natalie,' Sunny chipped in. 'She's worked as a stylist before.' This was quite true: the year before, Sunny had won a magazine competition and they'd all gone off to London to model party clothes for a photo shoot. Natalie had stepped in as an emergency stylist and she'd been great. She looked the part, too. Today she was wearing black low-slung jeans with a ripped black silk T-shirt, a red leather jacket and spiky red boots (half Goth). Jess could tell Murdo thought she was cool – and so did Bill. Josh had better look out!

'Don't you think it could work?' Jess asked Murdo.

'Guys? What do ye say?' he asked the other two Dogz. Sofa man nodded and meditating man was still on another planet. Michelle, Sunny, Caz, Lauren and Jess looked at each other, and waited. It was all up to Murdo now. Privately, Jess thought he'd be mad to refuse. This report could make Legendary Dogz look almost human!

'OK,' Murdo said eventually. 'We'll do it. But we're gettin' changed behin' the screen, an' no peepin'. Understand?'

Jess nodded solemnly, though she still felt like giggling. Legendary Dogz? This lot were more like pussycats!

From then on, things improved dramatically. Murdo and sofa man – Jess found out he was called Ned – had a heart-to-heart and settled their differences. Meditating man – Beezer – rubbed his eyes, drank a glass of water and came back down to earth. Lauren got busy with the iron, and Jess and Natalie put together all kinds of funky outfits from the wardrobe rail for the Dogz to try on: chainmail vests to show off their tattoos, studded leather fingerless gloves, leopard-print trousers, vintage T-shirts and shaggy fur coats.

Sunny had a chat with Beezer about Bombay, where he'd just been on holiday, and Caz finished tidying up. Michelle wanted to shoot off in search of Highway 101, but Bill insisted they all stayed put until the interview was finished, so she helped the camera woman prepare the scene instead. And Jess discussed with Bill exactly how she should introduce Legendary Dogz.

The band were great. Once they got the idea, they really threw themselves into the shoot, pulling all kinds of crazy faces and funny poses for the camera. Jess had to keep pinching herself to make sure she wasn't dreaming. Imagine her, of all people, mucking about with Legendary Dogz in their dressing room! Claire was just going to die of jealousy when she found out. Between takes, Jess told Murdo all about her annoying older sister and what a huge Dogz fan she was. Soon she was loaded with prezzies for Claire: a T-shirt which all the group signed (way better than a crummy poster), their latest CD, and then loads of signed posters for all of them. After all, they were fans now too – though Jess didn't know if she'd ever get to like their music. That might be a step too far.

At last the camera woman was happy with Jess's intro and her linking sequences (close-ups in front of the camera looking doubtful, horrified, approving, etc etc) and it was time for them all to leave. Murdo kissed everyone as he said goodbye (except for Bill), and Natalie took loads of photos. Everyone seemed to be delighted with the way the report had turned out, and Jess felt so pleased with herself. The fact that she was actually going to appear on television the next weekend was an added bonus!

However, once they'd emerged from the cosy dressing room into the harsh fluorescent lights of the corridor, Jess's mood changed. The others were chatting away ten to the dozen, talking over everything that had happened and pleading with Bill to meet some more stars, but she didn't feel like joining in. All those worrying questions at the back of her mind came crowding forward, demanding answers. Whatever could be the matter with StarStruck? Why had they ducked out of the interview? And what were the heavies doing outside their dressing-room door? Something had definitely gone wrong, and she couldn't go back to her seat without trying to find out what it was.

'Would you mind putting this lot in your bag for a minute?' she asked Sunny, handing her all the Legendary Dogz merchandise. 'I need the loo and we've just passed one.'

'Jess! We're about to try and meet Highway 101!' Michelle was outraged. 'Can't you cross your legs?'

Jess pulled a face. 'Sorry, I'm desperate. But don't worry about me – I'll catch up with you in a few minutes, OK?'

'Five minutes and no later,' Bill called, as Jess

hurried away. 'We'll wait for you outside their dressing room.'

'Sure,' Jess replied, quickly retracing her steps down the passage. A quick glance over her shoulder seconds later showed her that the others had already disappeared round the corner. Great! And, even better, the corridor outside StarStruck's dressing room seemed to be deserted in both directions. Although she had her pass now, Jess didn't particularly fancy a second encounter with that security guard. Especially not as she planned to lurk around, eavesdropping. Stealthily, she crept up to the dressing-room door. It was slightly ajar, so she put her ear right next to the jamb and listened.

'It's all very well, telling me to calm down,' a female voice was saying. 'You're not the one with her own personal hate mail, are you? He's not threatening all of us now, he's singled me out. He or she – whichever crackpot's been sending us these horrible poison pen letters. I tell you, Rob, this time I think he really means it. He's out to get me.'

'Look, of course you're worried,' came the

reply. 'Who wouldn't be? We all know how upsetting these letters are. But the place is swarming with Security and our bodyguards are on the case. We'll do our turn and then leave straight away. Whoever this nutter is, Shona, he won't get the chance to come anywhere near you.'

Jess couldn't believe what she was hearing. This was the last thing she expected! Who on earth could possibly want to hurt Shona? Well, it explained why there had been so many guards around the dressing room earlier on; in fact, she was quite surprised the corridor was empty now. Still, she could hardly march in and tell them to be more careful, could she?

'Maybe we should pull out,' another female voice was saying. This had to be Louise, the other girl in the band. 'I mean, if you really think he's planning to attack today . . .'

'But then he's won,' Shona said, sounding miserable. 'And it would mean letting down all the fans who've come to see us. They'd be so disappointed.'

Dead right! Jess thought, though she

immediately felt guilty for being so selfish when Shona could be in danger.

'I know these threats are probably just meant to frighten us,' Shona went on, 'but then another part of me thinks, what if he *does* decide to put them into action? What if he's got a knife? Or a gun?'

'Hey, you! What d'you think you're doing?' An angry voice suddenly boomed down the passage, reverberating off the walls.

Jess whirled around from the door to see a security guard rushing towards her. She froze, caught like a rabbit in a car's headlights, with no means of escape and nowhere to hide. It wasn't the same guard she'd met before, but this one looked just as fierce. She was in real trouble now!

And then, just when she thought things couldn't possibly get any worse, the dressing-room door was flung open and somebody reached out to drag her inside.

'I'm really sorry,' Jess said for the hundredth time. 'I didn't mean any harm, honestly. I just wanted to find out what was going on. You know, after the interview fell through.'

She looked around the ring of faces staring into hers and bit her lip, close to tears. This wasn't how she'd imagined meeting StarStruck. They all seemed so hostile! Jess had recognised everyone immediately, of course: Bryan, Marc and Rob, the three guys in the band, with Louise and Shona. Plus some others she didn't know: the heavily-built man who'd dragged her into the dressing room (Jess assumed he was a body-guard), and a few people looking after the band's make-up and wardrobe.

The boys were wearing jeans, combats and

cool T-shirts, Louise was in skin-tight snakeskin trousers with a cropped silver top, and Shona a white leather miniskirt. They looked even better in the flesh than they did on her posters – or rather, they would have done if they hadn't been glaring at her so suspiciously. And then a horrible thought crossed Jess's mind: surely they didn't think *she* was the one who'd been sending them hate mail, did they? She was the last person to do something like that!

'What was the name of that girl who was meant to be interviewing us?' Rob asked the bodyguard.

He ran his podgy finger down a list on a clipboard and eventually found it. 'Here we are: Jess Fitzgerald.'

'Yes! That's me.' Jess fumbled for her security pass. 'Look, my name's on this. I came with Bill – don't know what his last name is. You can check with him if you like: he'll be waiting for me down the corridor in a few minutes.'

Bryan took the pass, scrutinised it and then passed it around to the others.

'Oh, this is awful,' Jess muttered, half to herself. She appealed to Shona. 'I'm really sorry for hanging around outside your dressing room. I was worried, that's all. When you pulled out of the interview, I knew something must have been wrong and I just had to find out what it was! I can't bear to think of somebody threatening you. That's so awful!' And then she flushed bright red, realising she'd made everything ten times worse by letting them know she'd been eavesdropping.

Shona handed Jess's pass back to her – and smiled. 'It's OK,' she said. 'I believe you.'

Jess felt her legs turn suddenly weak with relief; she had to sit down on the sofa for a second to recover herself. Shona sat down next to her, and Jess really did have to pinch herself to make sure she wasn't dreaming. Shona Travis was about ten centimetres away from her! Jess had looked at her picture so many times she knew it off by heart; she even recognised the spiky choker Shona had round her neck. It looked just like gold barbed wire threaded with tiny stars, though it couldn't have been so scratchy.

'I love your necklace,' she

gabbled nervously. 'I've got a poster of the band on my bedroom wall and you're wearing it in that, too.' And then she bit her lip, wondering why she had to talk such rubbish at a time like this.

Shona didn't seem to mind. 'Thanks,' she said, touching the choker briefly. 'I like it too. This friend of mine's a designer and she made it for me when we started the band.' And then she went on to more important matters. 'The thing is, Jess,' she said seriously, 'you can't go wandering around on your own backstage. It could be very dangerous. For one thing, there's a lot of electrical equipment around and, for another, some weirdo is on the loose right now. As you seem to have found out already.'

Jess felt herself turning even redder. 'Sorry,' she mumbled again.

'Somebody broke into this dressing room earlier on today,' Shona said. 'What if you'd come trying to find us and bumped into him? Jess, whoever left that letter for me means business. You could have ended up in real trouble.'

'Now don't go frightening the poor girl half to

death,' Marc said, grinning down at Jess. 'No harm done, is there?'

Jess smiled gratefully back. She'd always thought Marc was the dreamiest guy in StarStruck; now she was sure of it! His hair was so dark, and his eyes were so very blue . . .

Louise broke in at this point before Jess could get too carried away. 'If someone's waiting for you outside, maybe it's time to get going,' she said gently. 'We have to be on stage before too long.'

'Oh, sure,' Jess replied, immediately scrambling up from the sofa. 'Good luck,' she went on awkwardly. 'I hope everything goes OK.'

The bodyguard began guiding her back to the door, but Jess felt she couldn't leave without telling the band what a huge fan of theirs she was. 'I think your latest album's wonderful,' she said, twisting her fingers nervously together. 'I've got everything you've ever released – all the singles too.'

'That's great!' Shona said, managing to smile though her green eyes were still troubled. 'I'm sorry you didn't get to do the interview. Here, let

me give you one of these.' She took a glossy hardback book out of a cardboard box on the floor. 'It's our story – all about how we got started. And I know you don't have a copy already because it's not in the shops yet.'

'Oh, thanks! That's great!' Jess couldn't believe her luck: Shona had found a pen somewhere and was signing the book for her before passing it on to the rest of the band so they could autograph it too.

'I'll keep this for ever,' Jess told them, holding the precious copy close to her chest as she was escorted out of the dressing room. She might not have been able to interview StarStruck, but at least she'd met them! And now she liked them even more than before . . .

Luckily, the bodyguard hurried away as soon as he'd handed Jess safely over to Bill, and she was able to make some excuse about having got lost on her way back from the loo. Nobody seemed to notice the book she was carrying – her friends were too busy swooning over Highway 101, and Bill was too busy chatting up Natalie.

'Rick actually kissed me!' Michelle told Jess dreamily. She touched her cheek for a second. 'I'm never going to wash again.'

'We all got their autographs,' Sunny said, waving her reporter's notebook. 'And Natalie took loads of photos. They were so friendly! I can't believe you missed out, Jess.'

'Oh, that's OK,' Jess replied. 'I'm not such a big fan of theirs. Come on, let's go back to the roadshow.' She was suddenly exhausted. Now was not the right moment to start telling her friends what she'd discovered and, besides, she wanted to hug her thoughts to herself for a little while longer.

They said goodbye to Bill and went back out to the noisy auditorium through a side door. Jess felt as though she were sleepwalking. So much had happened in such a short time! Of course meeting her pop idols had been fantastically exciting, and interviewing Legendary Dogz was more fun than she could ever have imagined. But everything had changed since she'd stood on stage in the glare of the spotlights, what seemed like an age ago. Somewhere in the middle of that cheering, noisy crowd was a person intent on harming Shona, and that thought terrified her.

They threaded their way back to Josh, who was grumpily watching Eastside strut their stuff on stage. Jess couldn't help smiling: he wasn't exactly a typical boyband fan and he must have been getting a few funny looks, sitting there on his own. But she couldn't give herself up to the music either – there was too much on her mind. Borrowing Sunny's glow stick for some extra light, she opened the book Shona had given her and read the inscription: 'For Jess: a rave reporter! We O U an interview!! Love, Shona XXX'

Maybe I'll take her up on that one day, Jess thought. StarStruck might be around for years to come, and who knew what could happen in the future. She flicked over the pages, fascinated to see how the band had looked in the early days when they were just starting out. Marc and

Bryan had such tragic haircuts, and Louise's perm was definitely dodgy! There was a picture of Shona at school, looking unrecognisable in her uniform, and a shot of her as Cinderella in the local panto. Here was the house they'd first shared together, and here—

What? Jess held the book an inch away from her nose and stared hard at the photo she'd just glanced at so casually. That was impossible! Surely, it couldn't be . . .

'Here they come,' Michelle said, nudging her. 'That dodgy band StarStruck, who can't be bothered to turn up for interviews. Hey, Jess! Where are you going?'

Still clutching the book, Jess had jumped to her feet and was blindly pushing past Michelle, Caz, Natalie and Josh to reach the aisle. 'I'll be back in a minute,' she shouted, though her voice was lost in the roar of applause that greeted StarStruck as they came on stage. She had to speak to them! There was something desperately important they needed to know, and somehow or other she had to get the message across – right away! This couldn't wait.

Rushing, stumbling, falling over her feet, Jess hurtled down the steps towards the stage as if a pack of wild dogs were chasing her. StarStruck had started their opening number. Their smiles were bright and they sounded as if they didn't have a care in the world, though Jess knew differently. She *had* to reach them – but how? A ring of security guards and crew stood around the base of the stage, scanning the crowd for any signs of trouble. As soon as Jess approached, a woman came forward to hold her back.

'You don't understand!' Jess shouted desperately. 'I have to tell Shona something urgently!'

'I'm sure you do,' the woman told her kindly. 'You and a thousand others. Write to the fan club, dear.'

'No! It's not like that!' Jess yelled, trying to wriggle out of her grasp.

And then she heard the sound she'd been dreading. A loud bang, followed shortly afterwards by another . . .

'Well, you have got yourself in a state!' the woman said, bending over Jess. 'That was only a couple of balloons bursting next to the mike.'

Jess picked herself up off the floor. 'I thought—' Then she stopped. It would have sounded ridiculous, saying she'd thought those bangs had been gunshots.

The woman began leading Jess away. 'I think you'd better go back to your seat,' she said firmly. 'We don't want to have to ask you to leave now, do we?'

'OK,' Jess said, realising there was no point in pushing her luck. She wasn't going to get near enough to the stage to attract the group's attention, and she certainly didn't want to be chucked out. She'd have to think up another

95

strategy. 'Sorry,' she added meekly, dusting herself down.

'That's all right, dear,' the woman smiled. 'You're just rather over-excited. Calm down and enjoy the rest of the show.'

If only you knew, Jess thought to herself. She walked a safe distance away and then glanced back casually to see if she was still being watched. The woman had gone back to guard duty, so Jess was able to lose herself in the crowd and edge back nearer the stage. Anxiously, she watched StarStruck perform. They sounded OK, but Shona kept on forgetting to smile and she was obviously having difficulty concentrating on the dance routine. Jess was still beside herself with worry. So the balloons had turned out to be a false alarm – next time those bangs might be for real!

Loads of people had got up from their seats and were dancing along with the band near the front of the stage. She stared at the crowd intently, looking for one face in particular. It would have taken too long to explain to any of the guards – and probably no one would have believed her anyway – but the fact was, she'd spotted someone in the book Shona had given her. Someone she recognised, though he wasn't a celebrity.

Just to make sure she wasn't imagining things, Jess opened the book again and hurriedly turned over the pages until she reached the right one. She waited until the powerful spotlight playing over everyone's heads swung her way and lit up the photo. There it was: that square, bony face with the thin lips and lank, dark hair. The security guard who'd hustled her out after  her first illegal trip backstage! It was definitely him. And then she re-read the caption underneath the picture: 'Backstage with Barry Westgate, the group's first manager'.

Jess closed the book and thought things over for the hundredth time. In any other circumstances, her eyes would have been riveted to StarStruck, but now she'd almost forgotten to watch them. She was certain Barry Westgate had to be the person who'd been sending the band threatening letters! OK, he might have fallen on hard times and started working as a security guard, but it didn't seem very likely. No, he'd been lurking around the corridors on his own at exactly the right time to break into StarStruck's dressing room. He'd have known the layout backstage, and he'd probably have been able to get hold of a pass and a security jacket easily enough too.

Plus, he had a motive. Jess was sure she'd read in one of her pop magazines that the group had sacked their first manager. From what she could remember, the case might even have gone to court. Hadn't he tried to sue them for loss of earnings? Something like that . . . and StarStruck had only become really successful after he'd left them. If Barry Westgate was jealous and resentful, he might want to terrify Shona and the others (to the point where they felt like pulling out of the concert) or even actually hurt them.

She shivered. Ugh! It was scary. That horrible man might be lurking anywhere right now, waiting to strike. She *had* to think of some way to tell the band what she knew – before it was too late. She wouldn't be able to get near them back-stage, not now she'd given back her pass, and she certainly couldn't break through the security ring while they were performing. Perhaps one of the guards would pass on a note? But that was too risky: she had no way of knowing it would get through. She had to talk to Shona face to face.

And then Jess remembered the arena's back entrance. Rob had said the group were going to leave straight after their performance. What if she waited for them there? Those girls in the Junior Journalist queue had told her that was where the bands came and went. Surely it was worth a try! She'd stay where she was until they finished their last number, just in case Barry Westgate showed his ugly face, then she'd rush round to the back and hope to catch them. It was her only chance . . .

'Oh, please let me through!' Jess begged, hopping around behind a group of slow-moving parents and their kids. It was just her luck to bump into this lot on the staircase! They'd obviously been waiting for the end of StarStruck's act too, before setting off on their mass expedition to the toilets like a herd of migrating buffalo.

'There's no need to push!' one of the mothers grumbled irritably. 'We're going as fast as we can.'

'Sorry,' Jess gabbled, seeing a gap and diving for it. 'This is an emergency!' If she didn't get a move on, StarStruck might leave before she had a chance to talk to them, and that would be disastrous.

Flinging open the heavy double doors, she ran outside the arena and skidded around the corner down to the back entrance. A flashy white Jeep with tinted black windows was being waved out of the performers' car park by an attendant. Jess stared hard, but it was impossible to see who was inside. And then she caught sight of the number plate: STRK1, and the gold star on the rear passenger door. It had to be theirs! Frantically, she waved her arms, trying to make the driver stop. There was no response. Whoever was behind the wheel must  have thought she was just another crazy fan.

'No!' Jess yelled. 'Please stop!' She held up the book, hoping against hope that it really was

StarStruck inside the Jeep and that one of them would recognise her. 'This is important!'

But the big white Jeep sailed past, leaving Jess staring after it in dismay. She set off in hot pursuit, still waving the book and shouting – probably looking like a complete idiot too, but there was no time to worry about that. Just when she was about to give up and resign herself to watching the car disappear round the corner, it stopped. And slowly began reversing towards her.

One of the tinted windows slid down and Shona stuck out her head. 'This had better be worth it,' she said, and Jess could tell she was only half joking.

Fighting for breath and falling over her words, Jess blurted out the whole story: how she'd slipped through a side entrance and tried to find the band backstage, only to fall into the clutches of this bogus security guard she now knew was the band's first manager.

'I saw his photo in the book you gave me,' she told Shona, riffling over the pages again. 'It was Barry Westgate, I just know it! And he was acting so suspiciously. He accused me of following him! Why would I want to do that? Please, you have to take this seriously!'

'Hang on a minute,' Shona said, withdrawing her head.

Jess could hear a buzz of voices from inside the Jeep, and then somebody laughed. Suddenly she felt very small and stupid. Why should StarStruck believe her? And what if she'd made a mistake, anyway? She hadn't seen the security guard for very long, and maybe he only looked a little bit like Barry Westgate: the photograph *was* rather blurred. She might be making a fool of herself for nothing.

One of the doors suddenly opened and Shona jumped down, followed by the bodyguard. She walked over to Jess. 'Look, I really think you should stop worrying about all of this now and just enjoy the rest of the concert,' she told her firmly. 'I know you feel involved and want to help, which is great, but you'll have to accept that the situation's under control.'

'Yeah, leave it to the experts,' the bodyguard added. 'We've seen enough of you for one day.'

Jess felt herself blushing, but then she decided to stick to her guns. Why not? She had nothing to lose. 'Please, just say you'll think about it,' she appealed to Shona. 'Don't you think it all makes sense? I mean, Barry Westgate would have every reason—'

'But Jess,' Shona said, beginning to sound impatient now, 'you've never met Barry, have you? How can you be sure he was the person you saw? You really can't go round accusing people without strong evidence.'

At that point, Bryan stuck his head out of the window and called, 'Shona! Get a move on or we'll be leaving for the airport without you.'

'I have to go,' she said to Jess, walking back to the Jeep. 'Sorry again – about the interview, I mean. Hope you like our next album!'

'Wait!' Jess decided to risk everything on one last try. 'He had a lisp,' she said breathlessly, hurrying after her.

Shona stopped dead in her tracks and swung slowly around. 'What did you say?' she asked, staring intently at Jess as though she were seeing her for the first time.

'He couldn't say his esses,' Jess told her. She would have felt a bit ridiculous if it hadn't been for the fact that Shona looked so interested. 'When he asked for my pass, it was like, "path".' And then she went on to imitate what the guard had said next: 'Thith ith a rethricted area.' She'd always fancied herself as a mimic, and that impersonation was spot on – if she did say so herself.

Shona obviously thought so too. 'That's Barry!' she exclaimed. 'He always thought we'd called ourselves StarStruck just to annoy him.'

Jess hardly dared to hope. 'So, do you think . . . ?' she began and then hesitated, waiting to see what Shona would say. She didn't want to jump to conclusions.

'Yes, I do,' she replied. 'I think maybe you did run into Mr Westgate after all. Jess, would you mind talking to our security staff about what you saw? It might mean you have to miss some more of the concert, I'm afraid.'

'That's OK. I don't mind,' Jess assured her. Now that StarStruck had done their numbers, she wasn't really bothered about watching anyone else. Except that it would have been fun to see Legendary Dogz, of course, now that she'd got to know them. And her friends would probably be doing their nut, wondering where she was.

Shona thumped on the side of the car. 'Guys, you'd better get out and listen to this,' she called. 'Looks like we'll be catching a later plane.'

And suddenly Jess didn't feel so stupid after all.

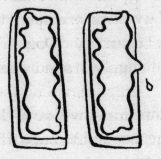

'Budge up!' Jess said, plonking a plate piled high with toast and jam on the coffee table and settling herself down between Lauren and Michelle.

'Great,' Michelle said, leaning forward on the sofa and helping herself to a couple of slices. 'I'm starving! You were such a pig with the pizza last night, Jess. None of us could get a look in!'

It was the Saturday after the roadshow and, because Jess was going to be appearing on television (yay! She could still hardly believe it), she'd been allowed to invite her friends round for a sleepover the night before, so they could all watch the programme together the next morning. Of course they'd stayed up really late that night, talking over everything that had happened at the roadshow, and now everyone

106

was still in their night clothes. Jess wrapped the enormous Legendary Dogz T-shirt more snugly round herself as she settled down on the sofa.

'Don't make a mess, will you?' Mrs Fitzgerald asked, poking her head round the door. 'You might be a minor celebrity now, Jess, but I still don't want jam all over my cushions.'

'Then let me have a TV in my bedroom,' Jess said cheekily – though she knew she was on to a loser there. Her mother was seriously anti-television.

'In your dreams,' Mrs Fitzgerald said, predictably. 'Give us a shout when it's time for your report. And you're videoing the programme for Grandma, aren't you?'

'Yeah, yeah,' Jess said through a mouthful of toast. 'Stop fussing! It's all under control.'

'You're getting above yourself, young lady,' her mother muttered, going back to the kitchen.

Jess wasn't too worried. She knew that both her parents were proud of her, although they didn't want to make too much of it in front of the rest of the family. The police had come to the Fitzgeralds' house on Monday after school, and they'd told her dad she was a very observant and quick-witted girl. Though of course she shouldn't ever wander round backstage on her own in the future.

Jess had had to tell the detectives exactly what she'd seen and heard at the roadshow. One of them wrote down everything she said, and then she'd had to read the statement over and sign at the end to say it was true. When she'd finished, the police told her that was all they needed; she didn't have to appear in court. Barry Westgate had confessed to sending StarStruck threatening letters and was going to plead guilty to harassment. There wasn't much else he could have done: the police had raided his flat and found some more horrible threats, plus a whole heap of cuttings and photographs of the band. He said he'd never really intended to hurt them but, even so, it was scary to imagine. Jess remembered how cold his expression had been, and how roughly he'd dragged her along the corridor. She never wanted to set eyes on him again.

'Hey! There's Frankie!' Sunny exclaimed suddenly, leaning forward to stare at the television screen. Jess was jolted out of her dark thoughts and back to the present. It was going to be so exciting, seeing her own face staring back at her from the TV screen! She would only be on for a few seconds but, even so, it was a big thrill.

'Just think, she was as close to you on Sunday as I am now,' Lauren sighed.

'I know,' Jess said smugly. 'I bet you're all dead jealous! Don't worry, I won't forget you when I'm famous.'

'Famous for what?' Caz retorted, whacking her with a cushion. 'Famous for stuffing your face with pizza? Famous for having the messiest bedroom in the world? Famous for—'

'OK, I get the message!' Jess tried to grab the cushion out of Caz's hands, though she was laughing too much to stand a chance.

'Keep the noise down!' Michelle grumbled. 'I love this song.' She took another bite of toast, wiped her fingers delicately on her Powerpuff Girls pyjama top and added, 'Anyway, I'm the one who's going to be famous first – everyone knows that. Josh and his mates are thinking of starting a band and he said I could sing with them if I wanted. In a year or so, maybe.'

Jess was about to make some joke about that, but then she bit her tongue. She could understand it if her friends were a bit jealous – particularly Michelle, who was so into music and dance. She wasn't about to start acting all big-headed about appearing on television or helping StarStruck. In fact, she'd decided to try and keep one part of the adventure a secret for as long as she could manage (she wasn't usually very good at keeping secrets). Upstairs in her underwear drawer lay a letter from Shona, thanking her for everything she'd done to help bring Barry Westgate to justice. She'd told Jess she definitely ought to think about becoming a professional reporter when she was older – she had such a good nose for a story. And along with the letter she'd sent a spiky gold star necklace, just like hers.

Jess had let out a huge shriek of delight when she'd seen it. Her mum had said the necklace might be quite valuable, but Jess didn't care how much it was worth. What made the present so special was the fact that Shona had remembered Jess liking her choker and had given her one exactly the same. It would always be a bond between them. Jess would treasure the necklace for ever, and perhaps one day someone might notice her wearing it and she would be able to say, 'Yes, this was a present from Shona Travis. She has one just like it.' Of course, they probably wouldn't believe her, but *she'd* know it was true . . .

'Hey, I've just noticed something,' Sunny said. 'Wasn't that Legendary Dogz T-shirt meant to be for Claire?'

'She's only gone and decided she doesn't like them any more,' Jess said darkly. 'Can you imagine? I give her all that stuff and she just chucks it in a corner and says she's into Tumbleweed now.'

'She's only jealous,' Lauren said. 'Is she still being mean to you?'

Jess nodded. 'I don't care. I'll get my own back, you wait and see.' She could picture the

111

headline already: 'My sister from hell! Famous journalist tells all!' Claire had better look out – she was keeping a diary from now on.

'And after the break, Legendary Dogz as you've never seen them before,' Frankie was saying on the TV.

'Mum! Dad! Come here! I'm on in a minute,' Jess yelled, diving forward to start the video recorder while her friends jumped up and down, screaming.

And she settled back to watch her first appearance on television . . .

If you enjoyed reading about
Jess and her pop adventures, look
out for other books in the Party Girls
series. And read on to find out how
to be a top pop fan . . .

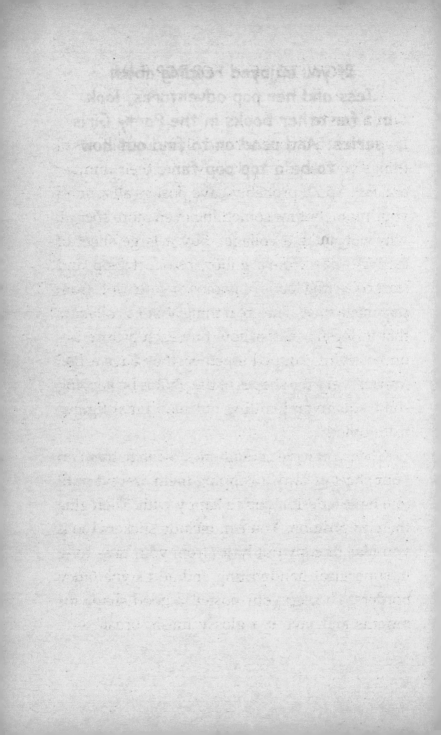

# HOW TO BE A TOP POP FAN

## Cut 'n' paste

If you have a favourite band, there are all sorts of things you can do to show you're their number one fan! You'll probably have posters all around your room, but for something even more special, why not make a collage? Buy a large sheet of card (A3 size) from a stationer's or art shop, and start collecting loads of photos of your idols from pop magazines. The great thing about a collage is that it doesn't matter how tiny each picture is – once they're grouped together, they have a BIG impact! Vary the shapes of the photos by keeping some square and cutting out individual figures from others.

When you have enough pics, arrange them on your sheet of card, swapping them around until you have a design you're happy with. Then glue them in position. You can include stickers too if you like, or copy out lyrics from your fave song in super-neat handwriting and add some fancy borders. To keep your poster in good shape for months and give it a glossy finish, brush on a coat of paper varnish (also available from stationer's and art shops).

You can cover books and files with collages, too – even furniture! If you have a tatty old table, desk or cupboard in your room, ask your mum or dad if you can transform it into something much more glitzy. First of all, rub the surface down with some sandpaper to roughen it so that the pictures will stick on properly. Then arrange your collage pictures and stick them in place with craft glue. A shiny border of sweetie wrappers looks great too. Collect lots of mini-chocolate wrappers, smooth them out and arrange them in stripes, with the same types together. (You can cover the whole table top like this, if you've eaten enough choccies.)

When your collage is finally finished, add a couple of coats of acrylic varnish to protect it. And if another band comes along to take your fancy, just stick some more pictures over the top and slap on another coat of varnish!

## Especially for you . . .

Another way to keep track of your fave pop stars is to put together a scrapbook or file about their music, their careers and their interests. Look out for articles about them in pop mags and newspapers, or on the Internet. You can add some more personal stuff of your own, too: maybe drawings or cartoons of your idols, or poems and stories about them. If they release a new single or album, make a record of its progress in the charts and collect any reviews – good and bad. And if you go to a concert, save the ticket or a programme to stick in your scrapbook so that the memories will come flooding back!

## Top pop gear

If you're going to see your favourite band live, it's fun to customise your clothes for the event. Craft shops sell glow-in-the-dark fabric paint, so you can decorate a plain T-shirt with loads of pop graffiti, stars and kisses! (Anything that lights up or shines in the dark will look really cool.)

Jazz up a denim jacket with press-on studs spelling out the group's name, or form it out of stick-on fake jewels, sequins or fabric letters (all available from craft or haberdashery shops).

Don't forget your hair, either – this is the perfect time to try something new! You could put your hair into loads of tiny plaits while it's still damp, like Michelle, for a crazy crimped look the next morning. Or go for two thick plaits and tie a funky bandanna across your forehead – or two high bunches that'll swing around while you're dancing. Bunches, butterfly clips and sparkly slides can make short hair look completely different too, so go wild and start experimenting!

**Rave reporter**

Finally, if you enjoy reading pop mags, why not produce one of your own with a few friends? You can decide on a name, design and illustrate your own front cover, and write all sorts of interesting features inside (nobody's saying they have to be true – as long as your magazine is for private circulation only!). You might like to include a list of fun pop websites, too. Or you could take a poll of your class and publish your findings on which are the most popular stars, radio stations or TV music programmes.

## On the net

Here are some cool websites you might like to check out:

### www.mtveurope.com

All the latest pop gossip, plus charts, competitions, and news of forthcoming events in the music world.

### www.kidscom.com

A great site with lots to do – you can record your own song and play it back, design party invites, make party food and enter competitions.

### www.foxkidseurope.com

Don't be put off by the boring home page – go through to the kids' site for chat, forums, polls and competitions.

### www.claires.com

All the latest looks, with some fab competitions to enter.

**www.dancingpaul.com**

This one takes a little while to download, but it's definitely worth it! Choose different tunes for Paul to dance to, select a background and make him groove to the beat. A real laugh . . .

# PARTY GIRLS
## *Jennie Walters*

| | | | |
|---|---|---|---|
| 0 340 79586 7 | Caz's Birthday Blues | £3.99 | ☐ |
| 0 340 79587 5 | Jess's Disco Disaster | £3.99 | ☐ |
| 0 340 79588 3 | Sunny's Dream Team | £3.99 | ☐ |
| 0 340 79589 1 | Michelle's Big Break | £3.99 | ☐ |
| 0 340 79590 5 | Nikki's Treasure Trail | £3.99 | ☐ |
| 0 340 79591 3 | Lauren's Spooky Sleepover | £3.99 | ☐ |
| 0 340 85413 8 | Caz's Confetti Crisis | £3.99 | ☐ |
| 0 340 85410 3 | Jess: Rave Reporter | £3.99 | ☐ |
| 0 340 85411 1 | Michelle: Centre Stage | £3.99 | ☐ |
| 0 340 85412 X | Lauren: Seeing Stars | £3.99 | ☐ |

*All Hodder & Stoughton books are available at your local bookshop or newsagent, or can be ordered direct from the publisher. Just tick the titles you want and fill in the form below. Prices and availability subject to change without notice.*

Hodder & Stoughton Books, Cash Sales Department, Bookpoint, 39 Milton Park, Abingdon, OXON, OX14 4TD, UK. E-mail address: orders@bookprint.co.uk. If you have a credit card you may order by telephone – (01235) 400414.

Please enclose a cheque or postal order made payable to Bookpoint Ltd to the value of the cover price and allow the following for postage and packing:
UK & BFPO: £1.00 for the first book, 50p for the second book and 30p for each additional book ordered up to a maximum charge of £3.00.
OVERSEAS & EIRE: £2.00 for the first book, £1.00 for the second book and 50p for each additional book.

Name ...................................................

Address ...................................................

...................................................

...................................................

If you would prefer to pay by credit card, please complete:
Please debit my Visa / Access / Diner's Club / American Express (delete as applicable) card no:

| | | | | | | | | | | | | | | | | | |
|---|---|---|---|---|---|---|---|---|---|---|---|---|---|---|---|---|---|
| | | | | | | | | | | | | | | | | | |

Signature ...................................................

Expiry Date ...................................................

If you would <u>NOT</u> like to receive further information on our products please tick the box. ☐